LADY WITH A LAMP

For over a hundred years Florence Nightingale (1820–1910) has been more than a national heroine. Her drive and energy transformed the Scutari hospital, which led to the recognition of the nursing profession and won her the title of 'Lady with a lamp'. Her famous story is one of faith as well as one of determination.

STORIES OF FAITH AND FAME

LADY WITH A LAMP

The Story of Florence Nightingale

by
CYRIL DAVEY

LUTTERWORTH PRESS
CAMBRIDGE

Lutterworth Press
7 All Saints' Passage
Cambridge CB2 3LS

British Library Cataloguing in Publication Data

Davey, Cyril
  Lady with a lamp : the story of Florence Nightingale
  1. Nightingale, Florence — Juvenile literature
  2. Nurse administrators — Great Britain — Biography —
  Juvenile Literature
  I. Title
  610′73′092′4   RT37.N5

  ISBN 0-7188-2641-8

First published in 1958 by Lutterworth Press
Reprinted 1957, 1958, 1959, 1960, 1961, 1973, 1977 and 1981
First Paperback Edition 1987

Printed by Cox & Wyman Ltd., Reading

CONTENTS

U.S.S.R.
CRIMEA
ROUMANIA
Sevastopol
Balaclava
BLACK SEA
Istanbul
(Constantinople)
Scutari

1

FLORENCE HEARS THE VOICE

WHEN the Nightingales' friends in England read the news they could hardly believe their eyes.

"The Nightingales have another baby!" they exclaimed. "Another girl, too."

"Fancy giving her a name like that! Did you ever hear anything so ridiculous! Whatever will the poor child do?"

"Did you ever hear of anyone calling a child by the name of the town she was born in? A town in Italy, too!" They looked at the letter to make sure they had not made a mistake. "Florence, indeed! Everyone who hears her name will laugh at it!"

No one could guess, then, how far that was from the truth. No one would ever have believed that the little girl born in Italy in the summer of 1820 would be honoured in every country of the world, or that before the century was over thousands of girls would be given the same name in her honour.

* * *

Florence was a year old before her parents came

back to England from Europe, where they had
spent the three years since their marriage wander-
ing round Italy and Greece. They could well
afford to do so, for Fanny Nightingale, Florence's
mother, had a good deal of money of her own, and
her father, whom everybody called "W.E.N.",
was rich enough never to have to do any work in
his life. It was just as well they were wealthy,
for Fanny had decided as soon as she was married
that she could never live in the old manor farm-
house which W.E.N. had inherited, and a new
house, Lea Hurst, had been built while they were
away.

Fanny looked at it in disgust when she reached
it. The footman jumped down and opened the
carriage door, the coachman leaped from his seat
to hold the horses' heads. Parthe, Florence's two-
year-old sister, was crying because it was cold and
she missed the sunshine of the Mediterranean, and
Florence herself, in her long, trailing clothes,
struggled in her nurse's arms to get down on the
ground.

"However do you think we're all going to get
into a house as small as this?" Fanny asked her
husband. "There are ourselves and the two
children. Then there is nurse and the housekeeper. There's the valet, the footmen and the
maids. How many bedrooms has the house got?"

"Fifteen," answered W.E.N.

"What?" snapped Fanny. "Only fifteen bedrooms? It's really quite impossible. We must have a bigger one. And a house in London, too. The girls have got to be brought up properly, not crowded together like people who live in cottages!" Fanny gathered her long, coloured skirts together and swept up the steps into the house. W.E.N. followed her more slowly, and the nurse, still carrying Florence and holding her sister's hand, came behind them.

* * *

From the beginning of her life, Florence was used to luxury. She could have everything she wanted, and there were always servants to do whatever she needed doing. Her father was a charming, scholarly man, who was always inviting wealthy and interesting people to stay, and her mother made sure that the girls were well-mannered and exquisitely dressed. Lea Hurst was kept for the summer and a new and much larger house bought in Hampshire, at Embley, for the rest of the year. Twice every year, the family went to London to stay for a few weeks. At Lea Hurst, in Derbyshire, and at Embley, Florence grew used to the sight of poor people, but none were so shabby and dirty as those she saw in London. Parthe would sweep her dainty clothes out of the way whenever they passed the cottagers so that they should not be

9

dirtied by touching them, but now and again Florence would stop to talk to them.

"I think it's dreadful that people should be as poor as that," she once said to her mother. "We have everything we want and they hardly get enough to eat. They never have nice clean clothes, like we have."

"Dirty creatures," snorted Parthe, wrinkling her nose.

"But *why* should people have to be so poor?" persisted Florence. "Doesn't anybody care about them?"

Fanny Nightingale put her arm round Parthe and drew her close to her chair. Florence always seemed a little queer to her, even as a child. She never wanted to be petted and hugged, like Parthe. "There's no need to worry yourself about *them*, Florence," she answered sharply. "God made some people rich and He made others poor. He knows why He did it and it is not for us to try and change things." She saw the frown on Florence's face and went on quickly. "You should thank Him for giving you so much when other people have so little!"

Florence's question was not really answered, but she said no more. She learned very quickly that her mother did not answer questions like that, and she gave up asking them. Instead, she kept her questions, as well as her dreams, to herself. In a house full of people, she was a lonely child, and though she played with Parthe, dressing dolls, putting them to bed and doctoring them, she never shared any of her thoughts with her sister. Somehow, she seemed to make a little world of her own, in which she lived by herself, right from the very beginning. She was grateful for everything she had—and to the end of her life she always demanded the best that money could buy—but she was not really happy.

*　　*　　*

Neither Parthe nor Florence went to school. Their mother wanted them to have a private governess, but none of the young ladies she interviewed were good enough or had nice enough manners. In the end, W.E.N. himself taught them languages—Latin, Greek, German, French and Italian—and history, while a governess gave them music and dancing lessons. In the classroom Florence was happier than anywhere else. She shrugged her shoulders when Parthe escaped as soon as she could into the garden, and stayed behind to read more history or learn more French or Italian. Over and over again, however, the same thing happened.

Florence would slip from the desk to the window of the "school-room" with her books. Then slowly the book would drop from her hand on to the window-seat and she would look out over the park, where Parthe was playing happily under the trees with her dolls. She would still be there when the door opened and Nurse came in.

"Miss Florence!"

Florence made no answer. She did not even hear.

"Miss Florence!" The nurse's voice was sharper and she crossed to the window. "What are you doing here?"

"Nothing. I've been reading."

"You're not reading now. You're day-dreaming. You're always day-dreaming, miss. It's very silly and very bad for you. Why don't you go out and play with Miss Parthe?"

Florence's pretty face grew sullen. "Because I don't want to, that's why!"

Nurse put her hand on Florence's shoulder. "Come along now, miss. You've been sitting here far too long by yourself, dreaming nonsense." She took no notice of the fact that Florence wriggled out of her grasp. "If you don't want to play, you should be doing something useful. Where is your embroidery?"

"I don't want to do any embroidery," snapped Florence.

"The devil finds mischief for idle hands to do. What will your mother say when I tell her that you're sitting here day-dreaming again?" Florence did not answer, and stalked towards the door.

"What do you dream about, anyway?" her nurse asked. But Florence left the room without answering that, either, and the nurse began to tidy up the room before she followed her out.

Scenes like that were always happening. If it was not day-dreaming it was "scribbling", which the nurse thought was even worse. Florence kept a diary, like most Victorian children, but it was not only in her diary that she wrote. Whenever something seemed important, she would jot it down on any piece of paper which was handy. It was a habit she kept to the end of her life, and there are hundreds of her notes preserved to-day.

Fanny found her impossible to understand. "I don't know what we're going to do with her," she would say to W.E.N. "Why can't she be like Parthe, a nice, polite, ordinary girl?"

"I don't know," replied her husband. "But it's Florence everyone notices. She's better looking and more intelligent."

"Oh yes, she's very nice when people are staying here. But they don't see her when she's disobedient. It's a pity she's got so much brains if it makes her bad-tempered. Anyway, who wants girls to be clever? Their place is at home, getting married and looking after their husband and their children. You don't need brains for *that*!"

W.E.N. laughed. "Oh, I expect she'll get married," he answered. "Before Parthe, probably.

The boys always look at her first when they have parties."

*   *   *

The years went by quickly, and Florence and Parthe grew into charming, gay young ladies. By the time Florence was sixteen Fanny decided that they must take a house in London for the "season" so that the two sisters might learn to mix easily and meet the best people. Embley Park would need redecorating, for a whole winter of house-parties would follow, and Fanny persuaded her husband to take the family to Europe for a year while the house was being done.

"It will do them good," she said, and added, after a moment, "especially Florence."

In the months that followed Fanny began to think her idea had been a good one. Parthe was thrilled at the idea of spending a year in France and Italy, and Florence, too, had changed completely. She was gay and happy, instead of being irritable and awkward. But the change in Florence had nothing to do with the trip to Europe.

It began in February. She had been reading and, as she often did, slipped off from the chair where she was sitting and went to the window. Her eyes had a far-away look. Nurse would have said she was day-dreaming again, though she would never have known that this was the most important day in Florence's whole life. She thought of Lea Hurst and Embley, of her friends and of all the happiness and luxury with which she was surrounded. She thought of the poor people she so often saw in the country and in London. She thought of boys she met at parties and of some of her older friends who were already married. What would she be doing this time next year? Or in two or three years' time?

Suddenly she looked up, startled and wide awake. She looked round the room, and then stood still as though she were listening to someone speaking to her. Once or twice she nodded her head, as though she were answering some Voice which no one but she could hear. Then, at last, she moved away from the window, crossed the floor, and went out. There was a strange look of surprise and happiness on her face.

A little later she wrote a private note and put it with her most treasured possessions. "On February 7, 1837," she wrote, "God spoke to me and called me to His service."

From that day she was different. God had something for her to do. What it was she had no idea, but for the moment that was enough. It was going to be many years before she found out what it was. She told no one what had happened, and her mother was quite content that she had changed into a gay and happy young woman.

2

THE HUNGRY FORTIES

THE door was open, but when the Nightingales descended from their carriage and rang the bell nobody answered it.

"It is the right day, at any rate," said W.E.N.

"And the right house," added Parthe. "120, rue de Bac. There it is on the door."

"Perhaps there is no one at home."

Florence stepped into the doorway. "Of course there is. You can hear them from here. It sounds like children, too."

"But Miss Clarke isn't married. Why would there be children here?"

Florence laughed. "I don't know. But I'm going to find out. If no one answers the bell, that probably means they expect visitors just to walk straight in." She pushed open the door, looked round the hall, and marched upstairs. "Everyone says Miss Clarke is rather—unusual." The others followed her, a little awkward and uncertain, and as they did so the sound of children's voices grew shrill and clear.

The Nightingales' tour of Europe was almost

over. Florence had been thrilled with the Riviera, captivated with Genoa and had fallen in love with Florence, the city of her birth. From Italy they had moved on to Geneva and from there, when it seemed likely that Switzerland would be involved in war, to Paris. The long holiday had gone on for a year and a half. At first Florence had wondered about her "call" and when she would know more certainly what it was that God wanted her to do. As she grew busier and busier with parties, concerts, receptions and operas, however, she almost forgot all about it. Paris offered more gaiety, and her last view of Europe before the family returned to a much duller life in England.

"You *must* meet Miss Mary Clarke," their friends told her.

"Why?" asked Fanny Nightingale.

"Because she is one of the most extraordinary women in Paris," was the answer. "She knows everybody. She dislikes women, as a rule, because she says they're stupid—can't think or talk sensibly and never do anything worth doing. But she has a great many men friends—important ones, too."

"What kind of men?" Florence had asked.

"Oh, people like Monsieur Mohl, for instance, the gentleman who is so interested in hospitals. He's always wanting to get more done for the poor people, especially when they're sick. Yes, you really must meet Miss Clarke. We'll persuade her to send you an invitation to one of her parties."

So it came about that the Nightingales were climbing the stairs to Miss Clarke's apartments, wondering what kind of person they would find. In the room at the top of the stairs they discovered two serious-looking gentlemen in black suits boiling kettles over an open fire. Beyond was an open door, and as they passed through they saw a riotous children's party in progress. In the centre was a lady, hopping and skipping in the ring of children. She was hardly any taller than a child herself and as soon as she saw them she called out to them.

"Come and join in the games!"

Florence picked up her skirts and flung herself into the dancing game while her parents and her sister watched. That was the beginning of one of the most important friendships in Florence's life. It was also the time when she began to think seriously again about her "call" from God. Talking with "Clarkey", as everyone called her, she shared more of her secrets than she had ever done with anyone else. When they left Paris for England, "Clarkey" promised to come and stay with the Nightingales as soon as possible. For Florence, she had a special word.

"Don't waste your life, my dear. You've got a task to do in the world. I can see that. Be ready for it when God calls you to it!"

*   *   *

Back in England, the girls found themselves caught up in a round of parties. It was hard to remember God's call when the London season was in full swing. Parthe could think of nothing but enjoying herself, and the sisters were constantly surrounded by groups of charming young men, in tight trousers, and gay waistcoats, with twirling moustaches. Many of them fell in love with Florence at first sight, for she was always pointed out as the prettiest girl in the room. Queen Victoria's wedding to the handsome, serious young German, Prince Albert, filled London with people, and the Nightingales were invited everywhere, even to parties and receptions where the young Queen and her husband were also guests. Life could not have been more exciting.

A letter from "Clarkey", about "women and their endless faddling and twaddling," stung Florence's conscience once more. She made a new friend who turned her mind to serious things again, too—the Chevalier Bunsen, the German Ambassador. The Bunsens had a daughter of about Florence's own age, and she was welcomed to their home. The Ambassador was a deeply religious man who, like "Clarkey", was interested in helping the poor and the sick.

"You should go to see Kaiserswerth sometime, Miss Nightingale," said the Chevalier.

"Kaiserswerth? What's that? Where is it?" asked Florence.

"It is in Germany, of course. A kind of hospital and orphanage and training place for discharged prisoners whom nobody else will help."

"It is run by Pastor Fliedner," put in Miss Bunsen. "One day I hope to go there and train as a nurse."

"I'd like to know more about it sometime," Florence said politely. "But of course my mother would never allow me to go to Germany, even if I wanted to. Certainly not to train as a nurse. Everyone despises nurses in England, you know. They're mostly dirty, drunken old women."

"I hear your hospitals are very bad, too," commented the Ambassador. "Dirty places, and very overcrowded."

"Yes, I think they are," replied Florence, "though I really don't know very much about them."

*   *   *

She was not really very interested in Kaiserswerth. She was becoming much too concerned about England, which was just entering on one of the saddest parts of its history. The "hungry forties" had begun. Ireland was already stricken with famine, and in England the price of corn and potatoes, on which the poor largely lived, rose higher and higher. Poor people, many of them out of work, could not afford to buy food. Wherever she went, in Derbyshire, Embley or London, Florence saw the same thing. Men and women, who looked more like scarecrows than living people, were begging for bread from door to door. Men sat outside their cottages because they had no strength to work in the fields. Now and again, as they drove down to Hampshire, the Nightingales' carriage was stopped for W.E.N. to give them a few coins, for which they almost fought.

"Poor creatures," said Fanny, with tears in her eyes. "I wonder God can allow such things to go on!"

Florence was just as full of pity as her mother, but for the first time she was beginning to see what God wanted her to do. "Clarkey" and the Bunsens had set her mind working in the right direction. At Lea Hurst she turned her back on the big house and went off to find what it was really like in the cottages. After her first visit she went again and again.

At first, she was horrified by what she found, and she never quite got used to it. She had no idea that people could be so poor, or that poverty meant that they would have so little. When she stood outside the first cottage door, she hesitated to go in, for the tiny house, with its one living-room, smelt stale and unpleasant. Inside, two children

looked up from where they sat on the unswept
floor. One began to cry, and the other clutched her
"doll" more tightly to her. The "doll" was a piece
of wood, with a bit of cloth wrapped round it, and
it was the only toy in the house. The place was
bitterly cold, for there was no fire in the grate and
had been none for weeks, though the windows
were closed and the broken panes stuffed with
sacking.

"Are you hungry?" Florence asked, and took
some bread from her basket.

The children leaped at her, grabbed the food
and, a moment later, were fighting for it on the
floor. A weak voice came from above, and Florence
turned away from the children, wolfing the bread
on the floor, and climbed the stairs. They were
slippery with dirt. In the room above was an iron
bedstead, a broken chair on which stood a chipped
earthenware bowl of water, and nothing else. The
windows were uncurtained, and there was no
covering on the wooden floor. The woman lying
on the bed, covered with a few ragged bits of
sheeting, was terribly thin, but her cheeks were
red with fever and her forehead was damp with
sweat. For a moment, Florence turned away to
hide the tears in her eyes. She almost ran down-
stairs and away from the house for ever. Then she
pulled herself together, and went across to the
woman.

"How long have you been ill?" she asked.

"I don't know. Days and days," the woman answered, weakly.

"Has a doctor seen you?"

"The likes of us can't afford doctors. Nor medicine, neither. They're for the rich, like you, miss."

"What about food? How long . . ."

The woman on the bed broke in quickly. "There was some old potatoes we bought, but they was mouldy. Since then, it's been any scraps we could find in the fields, or that people like you give us. My husband died two months ago, so there's no one to work any more. The children aren't old enough to work. The oldest is only four, miss."

Florence could hardly believe what she saw and heard. She crossed to the door. "I shall be back soon," she said. She paused before she went out. "Are the people in the other cottages the same?"

"All of them, miss. Yes. They say that people are starving all over England. Why should anyone care about the likes of us?"

An hour later Florence was on the way back from her own home to the cottages. She had clothes, sheets, food and medicine in the baskets she carried. It was the beginning of an endless series of visits to the poor and the sick in the villages round about. She had not heard God's voice speaking again as clearly as she had done a year or two earlier, but she knew now that He wanted her to dedicate her life to those who were in need, and especially those who were sick.

3

A SHOCK FOR THE FAMILY

"REALLY," grumbled Fanny Nightingale, "Florence is being completely unreasonable."

Parthe nodded her head in agreement. "She comes in late for lunch every day. And you can tell at once where she's been, by the smell. Down in the cottages!"

"I'm sure no amount of washing will *really* get rid of what she picks up there." Mrs. Nightingale wrinkled her nose in disgust, and looked at the clock. "There you are, you see. Half an hour late already, and she isn't even in sight." She turned back from the big windows which looked across the park, and took Parthe's arm. "Come along, dear child. It's a good thing *one* of my children has some respect for her mother. If Florence has no better manners than this we must eat without her. It doesn't seem to matter in the least that we have guests coming this afternoon. All she can think of is those dreadful people."

"And she never gives any of her time to me *at all*," Parthe sighed petulantly as they went into the big dining-room, where the maids stood stiffly by the sideboard, waiting to serve them. "She knows I'm delicate, and mustn't be worried. Why should she spend so much time with servants and villagers, and none with *me*? It's quite *hateful*!" She sniffled as she sat down.

The meal was almost over before Florence came in, washed and changed into a clean, rustling, silk dress. She apologised, but did not try to explain. She knew well enough that neither her mother nor her sister would ever understand what she felt. That was why she had never yet tried to tell them about God's call to her.

"Looking after sick people—especially poor people—is no work for *ladies*," snapped Fanny, watching the maid laying the plate in front of her daughter.

"But, Mother . . ." began Florence.

"I will have no 'buts', miss," cut in her mother. "The way you're going on is disgraceful. The whole district is talking about you."

Parthe's lip curled sarcastically. "I expect you'll want to be a *nurse*, next."

"That would be as bad as wanting to be a char-woman, I suppose?" answered Florence.

Fanny Nightingale rose from the table. "For a young lady of wealth and position, coming from such a house as yours, it would be a great deal worse," she said, icily. "But I do not believe that even *you* would descend to anything as low as

26

that!" With Parthe behind her, she swept out of the room.

Florence's face was white, but she did not reply. In some ways, she knew her mother was right. Nurses were mostly middle-aged women who could find no other work. Very few had any training, and hardly any of them knew anything about illness or its treatment. Only the very poor ever went to hospital, and the nurses' task was little more than sweeping and cleaning the wards, and trying to keep some sort of order in them. Many nurses were immoral and drunken women, and her mother was right in thinking that nursing was not a profession for well-educated, aristocratic girls. On the other hand, her friends "Clarkey" and the Bunsens put another point of view. "Clarkey" pointed out that some of the best nurses in Europe were Roman Catholic nuns, who took up their work not as a way of making money but as a means of serving God. Their hospitals were clean and well-run, and the "nursing sisters" themselves were good, highly-respected women. One of the German Ambassador's daughters was, she knew, planning to train as a nurse in the Protestant institution they had talked about. It seemed to Florence that what was wrong was not the idea of nursing, but that no one had ever tried to make it a really worth-while, respectable profession in England. Her mind was clearer, now, and in spite of the opposition she knew her decision would arouse in the family and her friends, she had almost decided that, somehow, she must become a nurse.

*   *   *

It was in July, 1844, that two important visitors from America came to stay with the Nightingales at Embley Park. They were Dr. Samuel Gridley Howe and his wife Julia. In their own country their names were already well-known, and while some loved them there were others who hated them. The reason was very soon clear to the Nightingales. The Howes were champions of the slaves, and were doing everything they could to help those who wanted to see every slave in America set free. Julia Howe herself was, a few years later, to write the "battlesong of the republic", sung by the armies who fought for the slaves' freedom—*Mine eyes have seen the glory of the coming of the Lord*. Florence found them two more people who had the same passionate love of needy people as "Clarkey" and the Bunsens.

"Dr. Howe," she said one evening, after they had been there a couple of days. "I would like to talk to you—privately."

"Why, certainly, my dear Miss Florence," said the doctor, in his rich American accent. "Anything I can do to help you I will. What is it about?"

Florence saw her mother rise from the piano,

where she had been playing to the guests, and come towards them. "Not now," she whispered. "I must see you alone. Can you meet me in the library to-morrow morning? Say at ten o'clock?"

Dr. Howe nodded as Fanny Nightingale sat down beside him.

Florence was standing by the table when Dr. Howe walked into the library the next morning. She looked young and charming in a long, gaily-coloured dress which almost swept the floor, but her face was serious.

"I'm sorry to bother you like this, Dr. Howe, but I want advice from someone outside my own family. Do please sit down." She indicated a large, comfortable chair by the fire.

The doctor sat down and looked round the lovely room, its shelves filled with books in many languages, most of them bound in deep brown leather. On the table was a huge bowl of flowers. He thought again, as he had often done since his arrival at Embley, that wealthy English folk lived in real luxury. They had everything that money could buy. No doubt this beautiful girl would soon be marrying some rich young nobleman and moving into a house of her own, and if she did, it would again be one very much like this. Perhaps she was going to ask him about some young man with whom she was already in love. He was all the more surprised at her first question.

"Do you know that the Roman Catholics have nuns—'sisters' they call them—who work in hospitals?"

"Yes," he answered.

"Do you think it would be quite unsuitable for a young Englishwoman to devote herself to the same kind of work?"

Dr. Howe looked up sharply. "Do you mean, become a nun?"

"Oh, no. Certainly not. I mean, do you think it would be wrong for a young woman—like myself, for instance—to train as a nurse in a hospital?"

"In England it would be very unusual." He thought for a moment. "I find that, in England, whatever is unusual is regarded by most people as unsuitable." His ideas about Florence had changed completely. She was evidently much more than a delightful and gay Society hostess. He looked at her serious face. "I see. You are thinking of yourself. If you feel that this way of life is the right way for you—go on with it. Follow your inspiration. Many people will criticise you. What about your own family?"

"They would think me worse than a charwoman." Florence smiled as she answered.

"Never mind. Go on with your chosen way of life, wherever it may lead you. And may God bless you!"

*   *   *

That was the turning-point in Florence's life. God had only once spoken to her directly, but she knew He had spoken through other people. She was certain that He had spoken to her through Dr. Howe. It was more than seven years since her "call". It had been a long time to wait, but now she thought she knew what God wanted her to do. The difficult thing would be to persuade her family that she was right. She believed that she knew the very man to help her in that problem.

Dr. Fowler, who was in charge of a hospital at Salisbury, not so far from Embley, was a great friend of the Nightingales and he was due to come and stay for a few days with them. He was not the kind of doctor who would tolerate the old, filthy hospital and he had plans for improving nursing conditions in the "institution" he served. Florence had more than once written to him about medicine and hospital work, for she had been reading everything she could find on the subject and filling book after book with notes, so that he knew of her interest and sympathised with it. She was sure that his visit to Embley would give her the opportunity she needed of settling her future and, with Dr. Fowler's support, she felt her family could hardly object.

Over dinner, Florence drew the conversation on to the question of hospitals.

"Really," he said, "it is not a subject to talk

about while we are eating. The patients are all pushed together in the same ward, in most hospitals. The walls have the plaster peeling off them and the floors are often rotten."

"How horrible," put in Fanny. "It makes me feel ill to think of them."

"I'm not surprised," went on Fowler. "There's not enough money to keep them clean—and in many hospitals the sheets are only changed once a month, no matter how many patients sleep in them!"

"But what about the nurses?"

"Why do you ask, Miss Florence? I'm doing my best, but it is going to be a long job. We can't get enough of the right kind of women, you know."

Florence looked round the table. Her father, at one end of the table, on which the silver gleamed in the lamp-light, was looking down at his plate. Her mother sat straight upright at the other end of the table, a frown on her aristocratic face at the mention of the forbidden subject. Parthe, next to Mrs. Fowler, shifted uneasily.

"I asked about them, Dr. Fowler, because I want to be a nurse. I want you to allow me to come to Salisbury and train in your hospital."

For a moment or two there was a terrible silence. Then Fanny Nightingale screamed. She went on screaming as Parthe leaped to her feet, put her hands over her ears and rushed out of the room.

4

NO. 1, HARLEY STREET

"I CAN'T imagine how she stands it," said Fanny Nightingale, in a shocked tone. She held Florence's first letter in her hand, and Parthe and W.E.N. sat talking about it in the drawing-room.

"Up at five o'clock in the morning every day," added Parthe.

"Of course, she often did that at home," put in W.E.N. "She found it the best time to study."

"Yes," said Parthe, "but she didn't have breakfast at a quarter to six!" She looked at her mother's shocked face. "And see what she says about the meals."

"They have four each day. . . ."

"Yes—but only ten minutes is allowed for each of them. And they only have broth and bread at two of them, and broth and vegetables at another."

Fanny shuddered. "She won't be able to go on like that. Why can't she remember that she's been brought up like a lady. She'll collapse—poor Florence!"

"I doubt it," said W.E.N. quietly. "And even

33

if she did, Florence would never give in until she had done what she wanted to do. There's more in her than either of you have ever realised." Her father had always been her best champion in the family, and understood her better than either her mother or her sister. "She has a spirit which will never be beaten."

*   *   *

Florence had not gone to Salisbury, after all. The Fowlers were almost as horrified as Fanny and Parthe at the idea, and the doctor did everything he could to dissuade her from her plan. Instead, she had managed to gain permission to go to Kaiserswerth, where Charlotte Bunsen had trained as a nurse. Her mother could not object that it was like Salisbury or that she would be working with undesirable people, for it was as different from British hospitals as anyone could imagine. Twenty years earlier a young German pastor and his wife had found a discharged prisoner on their doorstep. No one wanted him or would help him, so they had turned a dilapidated summer-house in the garden into a refuge for him. He was the first of many others. After the prisoners they turned their hearts to orphans, and after that to the sick. Now Kaiserswerth Institution included an orphanage, a prisoners' home, a school, a training-school for teachers and a hospital. It was clean, tidy, efficient and, above all, well-disciplined. The nurses were all good honest Christian women and girls, and the Fliedners made it plain that they all served other people because they loved God. Florence was intensely happy from the moment she arrived for, though she spoke very little about her religion, her own wish to become a nurse was simply a part of her love for God and her desire to do His will. She intended to stay three months at Kaiserswerth and then go home and make up her mind how she could best use her new training. It had not been easy to get her own way about coming to Germany and she determined to make the most of every hour she spent there.

When Fanny had recovered from her hysteria, after Florence had asked the Fowlers to let her join their hospital at Salisbury, she turned on her furiously. At first she accused her of being ungrateful for her home and the money her parents had spent on her. Then, for a while, she refused even to speak to her. Finally, she put her in charge of the store-room and the linen-cupboard, "to give her something to occupy her mind". The result was that Florence was driven to the edge of a nervous breakdown and had to go to bed for several weeks. Only when some friends of the family, Mr. and Mrs. Bracebridge, offered to take her to Italy, where they were going for a long holiday, did she begin to recover. Even then, it was not the thought of a holiday that helped her, but the idea, which she did not share with anyone, that she might persuade the Bracebridges to come home through Germany so that she might see Kaiserswerth, of which she had heard so much.

*　　*　　*

She did manage to see Kaiserswerth, but the holiday included a much more important happening than that. The Bracebridges had their holiday headquarters in Rome, where Florence loved to wander round the art-galleries, the streets and the churches. She came back, soon after their arrival, in great excitement after one of her expeditions.

"I met a most charming young man this morning," she said.

Mrs. Bracebridge looked startled. "I hope you haven't been speaking to any of these strange Italians, my dear," she said, sharply.

Florence laughed. "Oh no, he was English—very English. I could tell that as soon as I looked at him." Mrs. Bracebridge looked as though that might even be worse. "And he's married. Very gay—and interested in all things *I'm* interested in."

"My dear Florence. . . ."

"Don't worry! He's not only married—he has his wife with him. They are here on their honeymoon. His name is Herbert—Sidney Herbert. And his wife is called Elizabeth. She's lovely!"

Mrs. Bracebridge looked relieved. She was even better pleased when Florence introduced her to the Herberts, and wrote an enthusiastic letter to Fanny Nightingale about Florence's new friends. They met in churches and art-galleries, went for excursions together and arranged to meet again when they both returned to England. Florence believed her mother would be glad to entertain them, for Elizabeth came from a "good" family, and Sidney Herbert himself was a politician who was clearly going to be an important man in the Government. They were exactly the kind of people Fanny and Parthe would love to have at Embley—but there was one thing Florence did not mention about them in her letters home. They were just as enthusiastic as she herself was about improving the conditions under which poor people lived and suffered, and one of their special interests was hospital-nursing.

It was partly the Herberts' encouragement, and partly that of "Clarkey" and her husband Julius Mohl, which gave Florence the strength to make the final break with home and family and insist on going to Kaiserswerth for some training. The family gave in, reluctantly. God had not spoken to her again in the way He had done when she was a girl, but she had no doubt that she was doing the right thing, even though it strained her relations with her family. In 1851, fourteen years after she had first received her "call", she began her life's work.

*   *   *

If Fanny had hoped that working in a hospital would "bring Florence to her senses", she was greatly disappointed. When she came home from Germany she was more enthusiastic than ever. Fanny watched her walking up and down the lovely terraced garden at Embley arm in arm with Liz Herbert. Every now and again they would stop and Florence would point up at the windows.

"I see you are showing Mrs. Herbert some of the beauties of our house," remarked Fanny, when they met later in the drawing-room.

"No, not exactly," replied Florence slowly.

"Oh?"

Florence smiled at Liz. "No. We were planning where we would put the different wards if we could turn Embley Park into a hospital!" She almost laughed aloud at the shocked expression on her mother's face.

*   *   *

It was Liz Herbert who took the next step in Florence's career. Florence had been trying to get away either to Dublin or to Paris, to start some more serious training in one of the Roman Catholic convents, though she had no intention of becoming a nun, or a Roman Catholic. All her attempts had been foiled by sickness in the family, however, and it was only after three failures that she managed to break away from home and set off for Paris, where she was to start nursing with the Catholic "sisters of charity" at the Rue Oudinat.

The first night she was there, she went with the calm, quiet nuns round the wards. She was impressed with the quietness of the place, and with the peacefulness of the nursing sisters themselves. When she went up to the tiny room where she was to live—for she was not to mix too closely with the sisters themselves—she was full of joy. She knelt and thanked God that He had at last given her the chance of answering His call. Then she rose and began to get undressed. As she did so she noticed a little red spot on her arm. It irritated, and she rubbed it, without thinking. Then she noticed another—and another. When she took her dress off she saw that she was covered with them. She almost cried—and then sat on her hard bed and laughed at the absurdity of it. She was in Paris, about to train as a proper nurse—and somehow she had caught measles!

While she was still in her plain, stone room, kept apart from the nuns and the patients in case she passed her measles on to them, a letter arrived from England. She saw at once that it was from Liz Herbert, and expected that it would be an ordinary message of sympathy with some news about their mutual friends. It was nothing of the kind. As she read it, she knew that she would never complete her training in Paris when she was better. She would have to go back to London at once.

*   *   *

Liz had written to say that a new matron was needed for "The Institution for the Care of Sick Gentlewomen in Distressed Circumstances" in London. They wanted someone who could organise a big house, keep the servants and "nurses" in order, superintend the nursing, and who would be understanding with patients who came from very respectable families but now had very few friends and no money. Liz added that she was sure Florence was the very person for the post.

As soon as she had read the letter Florence knew that she would say "Yes". When she was able to leave Paris she went straight to London to look at No. 1, Harley Street, where the "Institution" was housed. It needed a great deal doing to it. She would probably have a lot of trouble getting the committee of ladies to agree with what she thought necessary. Suddenly, she wondered if she had not done the wrong thing. Ought she not to have gone on with her training as a nurse at the convent in Paris?

Just when it happened, Florence never told anyone. It was just about this time, however, that God spoke to her again. For the second time in sixteen years, she heard the Voice. It told her that she was right, and that there were still greater things to be done.

5

CALL TO THE CRIMEA

THE sound of the band reached the rooms of the ladies in Harley Street, and their pale cheeks began to glow with colour. There was something so exciting about it that their fingers beat out time on their white sheets. Those who were able to move about went to the windows to try and catch a glimpse of what was going on below.

Florence herself was excited, too. She went quickly to the door—now that she was the matron of the "Institution" it would not be dignified to run—and stood there with her nurses as the band came round the corner. In their scarlet and gold uniforms, with their huge silver instruments, and the big drum keeping a measured rhythm, they made Florence's feet itch to walk in step with them. Behind the band rode the officers, on lovely, high-stepping horses. Their helmets gleamed in the sunlight, and the long plumes on the helmets danced to and fro as the horses swung forwards. In the rear of the officers came the guards, and their brilliant uniforms, with their swords rattling at their sides, made a magnificent splash of colour in the drab street. Florence waved suddenly, forgetting where and who she was. She stayed there until they were out of sight, then slowly turned back to the house and her endless work.

*　　*　　*

It was the spring of 1854. These were the advance units of the British Army who were marching away to the ships which would take them at last to the Crimea, where they were to join their French allies. Very few people really knew where the Crimea was, except that it was somewhere near the Black Sea—wherever that was. Not many people knew why England should have gone to war again, after forty years of peace. All they knew was that war had broken out between Russia on the one hand, and England, France and Turkey on the other, and that their brave soldiers would soon be there to beat the Russians as, almost half a century earlier, they had beaten Napoleon.

Florence knew more about it than most people, and was more interested in what was happening. Her dear friend Sidney Herbert was Secretary for War, and Liz constantly told her how hard he was working at the War Office, and how worried he was about everything. But it did not seem to her that there was anything which she could do to help. The Crimea was far away, on the other side of

Europe, and like most people she imagined that the Russians would soon be beaten and the British soldiers back home once more. In any case, she had enough to do with her sick ladies at Harley Street.

*　　*　　*

The "Institution" had been in a bad condition when she arrived, and she set out at once not only to put things right, but to run it more efficiently and more cheaply. The day after she moved into Harley Street, she sent for the house keeper. As they passed by her door, the nurses heard two voices inside the room. One, Florence's, was so low that they could not hear a word she said, but the housekeeper's grew louder, and angrier every time they passed. At last, the door was flung open with a crash and the housekeeper flounced out.

"If you're not satisfied with the way I've been doing things I shall leave at once. Wages or no wages, I shan't stay where I'm not wanted," she stormed as she stood in the doorway.

"Very well," came Florence's quiet reply. "You can leave this afternoon. I can manage the house-keeping until I engage someone more honest."

The woman pulled the door shut behind her with a bang that shook the wall. With her cheeks flaming, she marched furiously to her own room. Two hours later she was gone.

That was only the first of a number of unpleasant interviews. The maids left, one after another. The house surgeon went a month later.

"I will not put up with laziness or dishonesty," Florence told each one. Her voice was very calm. She seldom lost her temper, but her eyes grew cold and her mouth set into a straight, firm line. Many people were to see her like that before she was much older, and there were very few who were able to triumph over her when she was sure she was right. The Ladies' Committee who raised the money for the "Institution" found her a very different person from the previous matron, who had always done exactly as the Committee had told her. Florence, on the contrary, expected to do what she herself thought best, and demanded that the Committee should back her decisions.

*   *   *

There was the day, for instance, when one of her Committee ladies drove up in her carriage and stopped outside the door. A footman jumped down from the driver's seat and opened the door, taking the lady's hand as she got down. The feather on her large hat bobbed about as she stepped daintily up to the door. She opened it and went in without knocking.

"Where is Miss Nightingale?" she asked the maid who came to meet her.

"In the cellar, ma'am."

The lady raised her eyebrows. "I don't think you heard what I said, young woman. I asked where I would find the matron."

"That's right, ma'am. In the cellar, I said. The coal-cellar!" She stepped back. "If you follow me, ma'am, I'll show you where it is."

"Nonsense!" snapped the great lady, pulling her coat more tightly round her as she came to the top of the cellar steps. Then, a moment later, she stood on the stairs in astonishment. "Miss Nightingale!" she called, "*whatever* are you doing?"

With a lantern in one hand, Florence was stooping over the coal, pulling it this way and that with her free hand. In her black dress, with only the flickering lamp-light in the cellar, it was difficult to see her. She did not even turn round for a moment, but went on pushing the coal about.

"I'm not satified with the coal-merchant," she answered, without rising. "Come here and look at this. He's sending us nothing but rubbish. I always thought he cheated us, so I've been raking all the coal over myself instead of letting someone else do it. I shall engage another coal-man. Come and look at it."

"I shall do no such thing," answered the lady on the stairs, tartly. "Look at coal, indeed! Look at my new dress, Miss Nightingale. It has got dirty already on your cellar steps."

Florence came up the stairs. "Look at my hands," she answered, thrusting her blackened arms out. "You can't do anything worth doing without the risk of getting dirty, madam." She went slowly into the passage and blew out the lamp. "And while you're here, there are one or two other things I want to talk to you about. I want a lift put in."

"A *lift*? Whatever for?"

"To take the food to the upstairs corridors. It gets cold while it is being carried up on trays from the kitchen."

"I never heard of such a thing!"

"No? You will, ma'am. They should be put into every hospital in the country."

"Is that all?" The visitor's tone was very cold.

"No. I understand there is some idea in the mind of my Committee that I am to take only ladies who belong to the Church of England."

"Of course."

"I want you, and the whole Committee, to understand that I shall take Roman Catholics and Jews and anyone else who is in need." Then, before the visitor could think of a retort, she smiled at her, gaily, for the first time. "Let me wash my hands, please. Then I want you to come round

47

and see what I have been doing to make the Institution the kind of place you want it to be."

*　*　*

Florence had her lift. She got better coal, cheaper medicines, better food. Before six months were over, she had almost everything she wanted, and the Committee not only respected her but backed her up in everything, while all her patients adored her. As the fight for improvements slackened, she had more time to think about what was going on outside, and more time to accept invitations to dinners and parties at her friends' homes. Before long, she was complaining that there was not enough to do at the "Institution". She wanted something bigger. She was sure that God had not called her to His service merely to run a nursing home for elderly ladies.

Now and again, Liz and Sidney Herbert asked her to dinner, but there was not much news about the war. The soldiers who had marched through London in the spring had not arrived in the Crimea by the summer. One day Florence came to see them in great excitement. Her eyes were dancing, and she could hardly sit still.

"Liz," she began, "I'm going to leave the 'Institute'."

"Why? When?"

"Oh, not quite yet. But I've been offered the

post of superintendent of nurses at King's College Hospital as soon as it is re-organised."

"How wonderful, my dear," cried Liz. "Now you'll be able to work out some of our ideas about training nurses properly."

"Yes. Isn't it marvellous? But I'm going to do a bit of *real* nursing myself, first. You know that cholera has broken out in the slums round Covent Garden?"

Liz looked horrified. "You're going to nurse cholera patients in the slums, Florence? My dear, you mustn't. Really, you mustn't. You may catch it yourself."

"I've promised I'll help, and I can't go back on my word. I won't come and see you again until the epidemic is over, though—just in case I pass it on to you."

There was no arguing with Florence in this mood. Liz gave up after a while, though she watched her leave the house with some anxiety. She wondered what news she would have of her. Neither she nor Florence knew that something much bigger, and much worse, than the cholera epidemic in the slums of St. Giles was just ahead.

* * *

The allied armies landed in the Crimea in September, 1854. It was almost a month later when Florence picked up her newspaper one morning. As she read, her face grew more and more serious. There was a report from the battle-fields, and it was almost unbelievable. There were 30,000 soldiers in the Crimea, said the writer, and all of them were as brave as lions. But before the winter was over, many of them would be dead—not from wounds, but from sickness and neglect. They were already suffering from cholera and scores were dying every day.

Florence dropped the paper for a moment, and thought of the people she had seen dying of cholera in the London slums. It would be worse on the battlefields. She picked it up again and read on. There were no spare tents, no real hospitals except a big Turkish barracks which was being used for that purpose, not enough doctors and hardly any nurses. What nurses they had were only soldiers, with no training for the work.

She jumped to her feet, and began to walk up and down her room. "Using soldiers for nurses, indeed!" she said to herself. "How stupid. They need women—trained women!" She stood by the window, looking out into Harley Street. "Some-one ought to do something about it," she said loudly.

"*You* must do something about it!"

Florence swung round from the window. There was no one there. The room was empty. Yet she was sure she had heard someone speak. She felt cold and frightened. Then her fear passed. This was what had happened long ago, and again before she came to Harley Street. God Himself had spoken to her again. Suddenly she knew why He had called her in the first place. Harley Street, to which He had sent her, had only been a preparation for the real work He wanted her to do. She went straight to the table, and sat down to write to Liz Herbert.

6

SCUTARI

FLORENCE'S letter to Liz crossed in the post with one from Sidney Herbert to herself.

"I want to take a party of nurses to the Crimea," she wrote, "and we must go at once." She realised very well that women nurses would be a completely new idea, and the Army authorities might not welcome them. In fact, they would probably regard them as a nuisance. She must have all the official backing she could get from the Government. "Would Mr. Herbert . . . give us letters of recommendation?" she asked, and went on to ask that he would write to the British Ambassador in Turkey. "This is not a Lady, but a real Hospital Nurse, and she has had experience!" Let him say that quite plainly. As she posted the letter she smiled to herself.

"Whatever Sidney Herbert or the Government may say," she thought. "I'm going!"

Her answer came almost at once. Herbert had written before he received Florence's letter. "There is but one person in England I know of who would be capable of organising and superintending a scheme for nursing these soldiers in the Crimea," he wrote. "Would you go and superintend the whole thing?" As soon as she read the letter she knew that she had not been mistaken. God had called her, from the days when she was a girl at Embley, to do this very thing.

*   *   *

She had written to Sidney Herbert on October 14, and told him that she proposed to leave England *in three days' time*. But not even Florence, with all her ability to get things done and get them done quickly, could quite manage that.

"You can't possibly get nurses together in a couple of days," Liz said to her. "Where are you going to find them? How are you going to get uniforms for them? And passages will have to be booked to France . . . and from Marseilles to Turkey."

"Very well," Florence replied, smiling suddenly. "Perhaps you're right. I'll wait until Saturday."

Liz laughed. "Florence, my dear! You're impossible—really you are. That's only a week from the day you wrote to Sidney at the War Office."

"It's four days later than I intended." She took a little book from her bag, filled with notes of things to be done. "I've got tailoresses making uniforms for the nurses already."

"What? Before you've chosen the nurses themselves?" Liz looked horrified. "How do you know the uniforms will fit?"

Florence laughed. Her beautiful, rather thin, face was alive with excitement. "We'll just have to risk it, and hope that no one is too fat or too tall to get into them, that's all. Anyway, Mary Stanley—you know her, don't you—is interviewing the women who apply to come with me, so it won't be long before we get the nurses into the uniforms and see for ourselves."

"What's the uniform like, Florence?"

Florence passed across her note-book, open at a page where there was a rough drawing. "There you are. It's grey in colour. A bit shapeless, I'm afraid, but we haven't got time to do anything beautiful. The dirt won't show so much on that colour—and there'll probably be plenty of dirt in the Crimea. There's a scarf to go across it with the word *Scutari* embroidered on it—that's the name of the town where the present hospital is, of course."

Liz pulled a long face as she looked at the drawing. "Good gracious! It looks a bit grim. Do you think they'll wear it? Nobody will fall in love with them in a dress like that, anyway!"

"The women I choose will wear anything, as long as they can work in it. And I'm not looking for pretty girls whom all the soldiers will want to marry. I'm going to have enough problems on my hands without that."

"I suppose you're right," Liz nodded and handed back the notebook. "Now, what can I do to help?"

"Make as many people as you can talk to believe that we're really doing something useful." Florence got up and paced across the room. Then she turned back and looked down at Liz Herbert. "You know why I'm doing this, don't you? It isn't just because I want to nurse wounded soldiers. *It's because I want to prove to everyone that trained and organised nurses have something important to contribute to the world,* whether they're in the army or in ordinary hospitals. Now I must be off. I want to see some of these women that Mary Stanley has sorted out for me."

* * *

The next few days were crowded. W.E.N., Fanny and Parthe came to London, all of them thrilled because Florence had become a national heroine overnight. The newspapers were full of her "adventure". But she herself had very little time to read the papers or talk to her family. She seemed to be in half a dozen places at once, and it did not seem possible that she even slept, for she was busy writing late into the night and yet was up and about long before most people were awake in the morning. At one moment she would be at the

War Office, arranging with Sidney Herbert for their journey across France; at the next, so it seemed, she was with the tailoresses looking at the dresses they were making; then she was back at the War Office arranging for money for the nurses' pay. Yet, all the time, she was meeting the women Mary Stanley had chosen, and deciding which she would take. In the end, she chose thirty-eight. Fourteen of them were professional nurses, middle-aged women of good character; the others were Church of England and Roman Catholic nuns, who had been working in convent hospitals or nursing-homes.

At last, Saturday came. Florence and her nurses boarded the boat for France, while a crowd of people stood below, cheering. They were a strange-looking group, the nuns in their long black clothes and the rest in ordinary clothes which looked just as drab. Each woman carried a cotton umbrella, which Florence provided for them, and a carpet-bag which contained their uniform, warm underclothes—and four nightcaps. The ship slowly pulled away into the English Channel, the cheers of the crowd growing fainter. Florence stood by the rail, a rather lonely figure, watching the white cliffs of England fading further and further away. The great adventure had begun.

* * *

A fortnight later, she stood by the rail again, as they sailed up the Bosphorus towards Constantinople. It had been a dreadful voyage. They had been welcomed in France with tremendous excitement, but by the time they reached Marseilles some of the nurses were already quarrelsome. At Marseilles she had spent every day—and night, too, it seeemed—buying stores, and seeing them stowed away on the ship in which they were to travel to Turkey. It was one of the worst ships they could have found, full of dirt and cockroaches, and pitched about so much in the Mediterranean that Florence was sea-sick the whole time. But now, at last, it was over.

One of her nurses touched her on the shoulder. "Isn't it *beautiful*, Miss Nightingale?"

Florence nodded. Constantinople, with its domes and minarets, was shining in dim sunlight. Round the ship were dozens of small boats, rather like gondolas, waiting to take off the passengers. But her eyes were not on the city itself. She was looking at a huge block of buildings, a little distance from the town, which she knew from the pictures she had seen of it was the Barrack Hospital at Scutari.

The nurses crowded round her, all talking at the tops of their voices. "Oh, Miss Nightingale," exclaimed one of them, "don't let us be delayed or held up when we arrive, will you? Let us get on straight away with nursing the poor wounded soldiers!"

Florence turned and looked at her. Her face was strained and her eyes no longer had any laughter in them. "The strongest of you will be needed at the wash-tubs," she replied, and turned away before they could answer.

*   *   *

The pathway to the hospital was rough, steep and covered with slimy mud. One or two of the nuns slipped and almost fell, but Florence marched ahead of them without noticing. A few thin, ragged soldiers watched them. One said something in a coarse voice and the others laughed. Nuns and nurses were going to be a joke amongst the soldiers, it seemed. At the top of the pathway, Florence stood outside the huge, forbidding building, waiting for her nurses to catch up with her, and for someone to appear and welcome them. Nothing happened. She led the way inside. The building smelt stale, damp and dirty, and her foot slipped on the floor of the passage which was caked with mud. A soldier in a torn red tunic came up to them and Florence asked him to take her to the chief medical officer.

The soldier stood looking at the crowd of women for a moment or two. Then he smirked. "We've 'eard about *you*," he commented. "You're not going to like it 'ere, you're not," he went on, in a cheerless voice. "The doctors don't want you. But you'd better come and see them, I s'pose." He led Florence away along the corridor. "The officers 'ave been talking about you already. They say they're not goin' to 'ave any women interfering with them and they won't even let you in the wards. Not that you'll *want* to go in them when you've seen them, miss," he added.

"Nonsense," replied Florence sharply. "We've been sent by the British Government to *help* the doctors."

"All right, miss." The soldier shrugged his shoulders. "You wait an' see, that's all. 'Ere's the office. You'd better see what they say to you. They'll send you back on the next boat, I shouldn't wonder!"

The man's words were only too true. The army doctors and officers had never had any women nurses before and they did not want them now. They made that plain to Florence as soon as she was inside the office.

Florence stood, as upright as any of the soldiers, and looked down at the officer sitting behind the table. She managed to keep her voice calm. "Very well," she said. "If you won't let us into the wards, we must stay outside until you need us. You *will* need us, from all I hear. At any rate, you must find us room to sleep."

"How can we get you in? The hospital is full of sick and wounded now."

Another officer stepped forward. "Major Smith has gone to Balaclava, sir," he said. "We could put them in *his* quarters. A bit crowded, trying to get thirty-eight women into four small rooms, with a pantry and a kitchen, but I suppose it can be done." The man behind the table nodded, reluctantly, and the officer went on. "I'll take them up there, shall I, sir? There's a dead Russian general in one of the rooms, but we can get him out after they've got themselves settled down!"

Florence shuddered and said nothing. She believed she would get more done if she did not argue, but only waited until she was needed. With her nurses flapping along behind her, she followed the young officer to their dirty, overcrowded quarters.

* * *

For four days they stayed in their rooms. Florence saw as much as she could of the hospital, though the doctors would not agree to let her do any nursing. She was horrified by what she found. The place was shockingly dirty. There were too few beds, and men were lying everywhere on the floors, groaning in pain. There were no proper kitchens—only a score of huge coppers, in which orderlies cooked great hunks of meat, which were chopped up on one of the beds at the end of each ward. In the same coppers the orderlies made "tea" without even cleaning them out.

"I know what you're thinking, Miss Nightingale," said one of the doctors. "We can do nothing about it. Believe me, we would if we could. But there's no money, and it's impossible to get supplies, workmen or anything else out here."

"But my nurses. . . ." Florence began angrily.

"Your nurses would only be a nuisance. They would be in the way of the doctors, and want to do all kinds of things which simply can't be managed. I can't imagine why Mr. Herbert and the Government sent you out here. They should have known better."

It was four days after their arrival that an orderly came to the nurses' quarters, to say that the Commanding Officer wished to see Miss Nightingale. During that time nearly a thousand more men had been pouring into the already overcrowded hospital, some of them wounded, but even more with cholera. Florence followed the orderly to the room where she had gone on the first day. The officer behind the desk stood up as she entered. He looked awkward, and asked her to sit down.

"When you came, Miss Nightingale, I'm afraid I was very rude to you. I told you we didn't need you or your nurses, and didn't want you."

"Yes?" said Florence. "Have you changed your mind?"

The officer coughed, and did not seem to know quite how to go on. Then he nodded. "I have *had* to change my mind. The job is too big for us on our own. I'm afraid I must go back on my words, Miss Nightingale. We need you and your nurses, after all."

7

LADY WITH A LAMP

"I TOLD you so!" The doctor stood still and took his companion's arm. "That woman thinks she's going to run the whole place!" he said, furiously. "Just listen to her!"

Ahead of them, Florence had stopped at the entrance to one of the biggest wards. Inside there were scores and scores of soldiers, many of them still in the uniforms they had been wearing on the battlefield.

"Why are all these men lying on the floors?" she demanded.

The doctors who were conducting her round the hospital before she set her nurses to work shrugged their shoulders. "What can we do? There are not enough beds for the officers, not to speak of the ordinary soldiers!"

"They will die of cold, even if they don't die of wounds."

"I'm afraid you're quite right, Miss Nightingale. But we can't do anything about it. There aren't enough blankets to keep them warm, and we can't get any more."

"What about operations?"

"We have to do them in the wards, of course."

Florence shuddered. "With all the rest of the sick men looking on?"

"Certainly. There are not enough rooms for the men who are sick. We have none to spare for operating-theatres." The doctor who was speaking looked helpless. "There aren't even any operating-tables. We have to use ordinary ones. Ever since the war began we have been making do with what we can get." He turned back into the corridor. "I will *not* have you arguing with me in front of those men, Miss Nightingale."

"Have you enough anæsthetics?"

"Anæsthetics? We have none at all. When a man has his leg cut off he simply has to grin and bear it."

Florence stopped in the middle of the wet, dirty corridor. Her beautiful face was white. She controlled her voice when she spoke, but it beat about the doctors like a whip. "I have never heard anything so disgraceful in my life. *Why* is everything in this state?" she demanded. "*Why* are there no anæsthetics? *Why* aren't the wards and corridors scrubbed? *Why* haven't these wounded men got clean clothes? Why must they lie in the filthy uniforms and muddy blankets they wore in the battlefields?"

The doctors waited for their chief to answer.

When he did so his voice, too, was calm, though he looked as red as the uniform he wore. "Miss Nightingale," he said, "you are a woman. You know nothing about war or about the army. That is why we didn't want you or your nurses here. We knew you would do nothing but criticise. It is impossible to expect women to put up with conditions like these. I admit that. *We're* used to it. You'd better get your nurses together and take the first ship back to England that you can find." He turned on his heel, and began to walk away, but Florence's next words brought him to a stop.

"I am *not* going back to England," she said clearly. "And I do not propose to put up with these conditions. I have been sent by the Government to superintend the nursing of these wounded and sick men, and I am going to start *now*."

"But . . ." began the doctor, while his colleagues stared at her.

"Have you any soldiers who can scrub floors?" she asked, without waiting for him to finish.

"Scrub? Yes, I suppose so. But we haven't any scrubbing brushes."

"And no money to buy any," put in another doctor. "That's why there is all this confusion. That's why there are no blankets or operating tables. The Army won't give us money to buy them."

Florence's answer took their breath away. *"I*

have the money, gentlemen," she said. "We won't worry about the Army."

"But . . ." began one of the officers again.

Florence cut in on his question. "Don't you realise that people in England have been giving money to provide comforts for these men? And that I collected a great deal myself?" She did not tell them she had £30,000 to spend as she found necessary. "I want two or three men to come with me into Constantinople to buy scrubbing brushes. Two hundred should be enough to begin with, don't you think?"

"Two hundred *scrubbing-brushes*?" The senior officer gasped.

"After that we must deal with operations. Men *can't* be allowed to watch. I will see that screens are bought. How many operating-tables will you need? Half a dozen to begin with, I think?"

"Er . . . yes, of course." The officers and doctors standing round her were gaping at this young and charming lady who seemed so full of authority. "We shall need soap if the floors are to be scrubbed, ma'am," said one of them, weakly.

Florence smiled suddenly, for the first time, and the officers saw the hardness melt from her face. All at once they realised that they were not only in the presence of a great, hard-driving genius, but of a very lovely lady. "Women don't forget soap, sir," she answered. "Especially well-brought-up nurses.

They smell it too often!" She brought out a little notebook from one of her pockets. "Look! There it is—under the word scrubbing-brushes."

They noticed that below that was a long list. "Are there other things you propose to buy for the hospital, ma'am?" asked one of them.

"Shirts. Socks. Underclothes. Blankets." Florence was reading her list through quickly, aloud. "Trays. Tables. Clocks. Forks. Spoons. Plates. They're all here, gentlemen. We shall get them as soon as we can. Some of them I have already in my own baggage. I bought them in Marseilles, just in case they were needed. The others we should be able to buy in Constantinople. I hope that in, say, six weeks, we shall have everything you want." She smiled at them again, and walked away towards her own quarters.

*   *   *

That was their first sight of what the Army soon began to call "the Nightingale power". Florence kept her word. In less than two months, there were very few things missing in the wards. Some of the senior officers feared her, and even hated her, making her work as difficult as possible, but nothing could stop her. She opened empty blocks of the barracks, and hired Turkish workmen to clean them out. She saw a new regiment of soldiers arrive wearing tropical clothing in the midst of

winter, because the Army had no more warm
uniforms to issue, and went into Constantinople
and refitted the whole regiment with clothing
which she bought there. There seemed nothing
that she could not do. Nothing was too much
trouble, if it brought help and comfort to the sick
and wounded soldiers. She seemed to have energy
that could not be exhausted. All day long she was
walking round the hospital, superintending the
work of the nurses, and every night a light burned
in her room until the early hours of the morning
as she wrote long letters and reports to Sidney
Herbert at the War Office, urging him to do more
and more for the men in the Crimea.

*   *   *

The patients in the huge hospital had no idea of
all this work, though they knew that as soon as she
had arrived things had begun to happen. To them
she was "the lady with a lamp".

Three months after her arrival in the Crimea
there were more men in hospital than in the army
besieging Sevastopol. Many of them poured into
Scutari. They lay in the wards, and along the
corridors because there was no more room inside
the wards. There were often too many for the
doctors to deal with, but every day and every
night Florence passed round the whole hospital.

A new patient, looking round the ward, saw that

everyone was watching the door. "What are they all waiting for, mate?" he asked the soldier in the next bed.

"Waiting for Miss Nightingale, of course," was the answer. "Look! She's coming!"

The door had opened, and Florence came in, followed by a doctor, who made notes as she spoke to each man. "She can't go to *every* bed," thought the new-comer, but that was exactly what she did. Then she was by his own bedside, looking down at him.

"What is your name?" she asked. "You came in to-day, didn't you?"

"Joe," he said shyly. "Joe Grimes, miss." He looked up at her. She was wearing a grey uniform, with a scarf across her breast embroidered with the word *Scutari*. Her cap did not hide her brown hair, and he thought her face was the kindest he had ever seen. "Got hit by a cannon ball, I did, miss—outside Sevastopol." He was in pain, and his face twisted with agony. He was only a boy, not much more than seventeen, and suddenly he blurted out the truth. "I'm frightened, miss." He thought she would laugh at him, a soldier, for admitting anything so silly.

"Frightened of the operation? You know the doctor says he will have to take your leg away, don't you? Most of the men are frightened when they think of the operation, Joe—that's nothing to be ashamed of. Do you want me to stand by you when they do it? I will come if it will help you. That's why I'm here—to help you."

Joe could only nod. When she had passed on down the ward he turned to the man in the next bed. "I've never seen anyone as kind as that. And she's beautiful, too, ain't she? She looked at me as if she *cared* about me." His leg hurt again, and he began to cry quietly to himself.

That was the greatest thing about Florence. She *did* care about them. She wrote letters for them, talked to them, advised them, comforted them when they were weak or suffering, and sat by them when they were dying. If it was important in the daytime, it was even more important at night.

*   *   *

Joe Grimes lay in his hard, iron bed that night, sweating with pain. Here and there a man groaned, and all over the ward men could be heard turning and twisting. He remembered how Florence had kept her word in the afternoon. Two orderlies had lifted him out of bed on to a rough stretcher, carried him along the ward and into another one. Across one corner there were screens. He was taken behind them and as soon as he saw the operating table, he began to try and struggle off the stretcher. A doctor had his back to him, and

Joe knew that he was looking over the instruments for the operation. Then, before he could shout, he felt a hand on his arm and, looking up, he saw Florence.

"Do you want me to stay with you?" she asked. He nodded. "Then you must promise to be good. No shouting, even when it hurts." She smiled down at him. He took her hand. Through the whole operation he never made a sound, though he bit his lip harder and harder. For nearly an hour Florence stood by him, holding his hand until it was all over.

Now, Joe was lying in the dark, knowing that he would never be able to walk or run properly again. There was a sound at the end of the ward. The door opened, and a ray of light shone into the darkness. It shone on to a grey uniform. The light came down the ward, very slowly, stopping at the foot of every bed. Now and again, he saw that it was put on the floor for a moment. Then, throwing huge shadows on the wall, the lady with the lamp reached his bed.

"Are you asleep, Joe?"

He could hardly believe it. She remembered his bed, and his name. "No, miss," he replied.

She put the lamp on the floor and sat beside him, taking his hand again. Then she moved the blankets, looked at his leg, loosened the bandage a little in one place and tied it more tightly in another. "Is that better?" she asked. Then she picked up the lamp and went on, down the ward. Joe watched the light, and the shadows, as she went on, stopping every now and again where a man was awake. He knew now that she would do this every night. In every part of the hospital the lamp would shine for a few minutes, lighting up her face. Perhaps she would get a few hours' sleep, perhaps she would sit for the whole night by the bed of a man who was dying. She would go on, and on, and on, until the war was over or she herself collapsed with weariness. Joe knew that he would remember that light moving up and down the ward as long as he could remember anything. It was as though Jesus Himself were walking round the wards. For the first time for many months he tried to pray, to thank God for the love and care of the lady with a lamp.

In every ward and every corridor of Scutari Hospital men watched and waited for her to come, and when she had gone, thanked God for what she had done.

8

FLORENCE WINS HER FIGHT

AT Balaclava, the skies were blue. Spring was in the air, and some of the winter's misery had been forgotten. The soldiers were moving about their tents in the huge camp, cleaning guns and uniforms, and resting after their last battle with the Russians. Suddenly one of the men looked up and shouted to his friends, pointing to the edge of the camp.

A troop of horsemen was riding in. The gold braid of the officers shone in the sunlight, and their brilliant uniforms stood out vividly against the dull, patched tents. The tall plumes on the horsemen's helmets quivered in the breeze, and their horses stepped carefully over the muddy, congested ground. Then they saw something else that was even more astonishing than this colourful procession itself. Riding in the midst of it was a lady, dressed in black, sitting upright on her side-saddle.

The soldiers looked more closely. Some of them had been in hospital at Scutari. All at once, they remembered the lady in grey who had walked the wards so untiringly, the lady with a lamp. They shouted again to their comrades, and ran from tent to tent, as the horsemen advanced. Then the air was shattered by a cheer. The shouting grew in volume, and went on and on, as more and more men heard that Florence Nightingale herself was in Balaclava. They crowded round the horses, until it was impossible for them to move any further. Hats were flung into the air and the crowd grew denser as men rushed from all parts of the camp. It was the biggest welcome Florence had ever received.

From the group of horsemen a little, tubby man with a black beard leapt off his horse, chattering excitedly. It was Alexis Soyer, the French chef who had come to organise the kitchens at Scutari because he had heard so much of Florence and her work. Rushing to her horse, he almost pulled her off it. Then, gathering her in his arms, he heaved her up on top of a cannon, where she could be seen by everyone. He began to make a long speech, chattering in French and waving his arms in all directions. No one understood, and no one listened. The soldiers went on cheering. Florence had come, for the first time, to the battlefield.

*　　*　　*

This welcome from the soldiers was one of the few bright things about her visit, and made up for some of the misery of the last months at Scutari. As winter came, conditions in the Crimea had grown worse and worse. Men crowded the hospital to overflowing. There was food enough for them, and Florence had managed to get medical supplies and blankets, but the dreadful thing was the cold. She had never known a winter like it. The ground was covered with snow, frozen hard. Every night the thermometer was well below freezing-point and sometimes it remained there day after day. It was hardly possible to get enough fuel to keep the fires going under the kitchen stoves. The men who were well enough to do so went out to try and gather what they could find, but almost always they came back empty-handed. The cooks came to her in despair.

"We've been promised some fuel for the day after to-morrow, miss," they said.

"What about to-day?"

The men shrugged their shoulders. "There's nothing to burn. Whatever they have in the wards, it will have to be cold."

Florence whipped round on the officer standing by. "The seriously-ill men *must* have warm soup, at least. Otherwise they will die."

"Then they'll have to die, that's all," answered the officer. "I've done everything I can. I've done my best. We have nothing to burn, Miss Nightingale. *Nothing*. Surely you understand that?"

"Come with me," Florence said to the soldiers. The officer followed her to the nearest ward. She went to the curtained portion at the end. A doctor was standing by the operating table. "Take this away and chop it up!" she ordered. The men stood, gaping. "Did you hear what I said? Take this table and use it for the fires. I will give you some more when you've used this one."

As the men picked it up the doctor sprang forward. "You can't *do* that," he shouted. "Where am I going to operate?"

"On the floor," she answered, "or on one of the beds."

"Impossible. You can't burn the operating tables!"

"I can," said Florence, "and I will. *I* bought the operating tables, not the Army. I will see that you have some more as soon as possible. Some of the men will die if they are not operated on, but a great many more will die unless they have hot soup and drink. Be careful with it," she added to the kitchen-orderlies. "Make it go as far as you can." She followed them out, leaving the doctor muttering under his breath.

* * *

It had gone on like that all winter. Florence spent more and more money and, although she often seemed hard and even ruthless, doctors and

officers supported her and loved her as much as
the men lying sick in the wards. It was impossible
to imagine what the hospital would have been like
without her. Then, as soon as the spring came,
she determined to see what could be done for the
other hospitals in the battlefields themselves. She
set off for Sevastopol and Balaclava.

After her terrific welcome from the soldiers she
jumped down from the cannon and asked to be
taken to the hospital. She was horrified by what
she saw. There were few stores, hardly any
medical supplies or medicine, a few overworked
nurses. No one in authority seemed able to do
anything or to care what happened. They had
given up in despair. She walked through the
hospital-tents and huts, her face growing colder
and angrier as she went on. The medical officers
watched her and said nothing until she turned to
them.

"This is dreadful. No wonder men die here! It
is disgusting."

The doctors shrugged their shoulders. "It is
the best we can do."

"Nonsense," answered Florence. "Use your
imagination. The place could be clean, at any
rate." She paused and looked round. "I shall see
to it myself."

Dr. John Hall, the Chief Medical Officer in the
Crimea, grew red in the face. "You will do nothing

of the kind, Miss Nightingale," he snapped. "They may put up with your bossing them about in Scutari, but you will do what you're told here. *I* am in command here, and I will not tolerate your orders or your presence. You will not come into these hospitals again without my permission—and that is one thing you will never get!" He glared at her. "Now, if you please, you will get out—at once!"

Florence spent no time in arguing. She had no doubt that in the end she would win her fight here in the Crimea itself, as she had done in Constantinople, but it would take time. She must write to Sidney Herbert, and ask him to send a letter from the War Office to Dr. Hall. Back in her tent she sat down to compose her letter.

* * *

Only a couple of days later a dreadful rumour began to pass round the camp. A great silence settled over the tents, and the soldiers went slowly about their work. It was almost as if the whole war had been lost.

"Miss Nightingale is dead!"

The rumour sped round the camp and back to Scutari. Soldiers began their letters home with it and the news spread round England. It was not true, but it was not far from the truth. Florence had, in fact, caught the dreaded "Crimea fever" when she visited the hospitals and was so seriously ill that the doctors thought she could not live. The long months of worry and overwork had weakened her so that she had hardly any strength left. The camps were silent. In England, people stopped strangers in the street to ask if there was any news of her. Two or three times a day, Queen Victoria herself sent to Sidney Herbert for news.

A fortnight after she fell ill, a horseman wrapped in a long, dark cloak reined in at the door of the hut where she lay.

"I have come to see Miss Nightingale," he said to the nurse who came to the door.

The woman looked at him in astonishment. "No one can see Miss Nightingale," she answered. "You ought to know that. I doubt if the doctors would even let the Commander-in-Chief himself see her."

The horseman flung open his cloak. His scarlet, gold and blue uniform almost dazzled the nurse. "We must ask them. I am Lord Raglan, the Commander-in-Chief."

For a while he was allowed to sit by her bedside. She smiled at him and tried to talk, until the doctors stopped her. That night Lord Raglan telephoned to London that Florence had passed the crisis of her fever and was going to recover.

*   *   *

Getting better took a long time, but she was encouraged by many things. The love of the soldiers, the long letters from friends at home, the interest of Queen Victoria who asked Sidney Herbert to send her a message thanking her for all her work and, above all, an "order of the day" which was sent to every regiment in the Army and to the doctors in the Crimea that she was in command of all the nurses' services and no one was to hinder her work in any way—these things all helped her to recover. As soon as she was convalescent, she began work again, writing letters and reports, seeing doctors and nurses and giving orders. As soon as she was able to get out again a special carriage was given her to ride in, so that she might not tire herself out on horseback. The worst part of her work was over.

There were other worries, however, both about the nurses and the soldiers. One afternoon, there was a knock at the door of her room.

"Come in," she called.

A sergeant entered. "I've come to see you, miss," he said awkwardly.

"I can see that," answered Florence tartly. "What is it?"

"I want to marry one of the nurses," he began.

Florence got up from her chair. "My dear young man," she said. "You're the fourth soldier this morning who has come to see me about marrying one of my nurses. I only hope you don't all want to marry the same one. Listen to me, Sergeant. My nurses came to the Crimea to nurse, not to get married. When they are back in England and you are there, too, you can do what you like, but while they are here, my nurses are going to *nurse*!"

Even that was not as bad as the Turkish gentleman who came and asked her if he could buy one of the stoutest of her nurses.

"*Buy* her?" exclaimed Florence, in astonishment. "Whatever for?"

"For my wife, ma'am," he explained.

"But have you no wife already?"

"Why, yes," he said. "But I would like another one. I have only three, and none are as fat as she is!"

*　*　*　*

For the rest of her time in the Crimea Florence worked less in the hospitals, which were now well organised, and more in trying to help the soldiers in their spare time. She had the beer-shops closed, and opened schools and coffee-houses instead. She worked out a way in which soldiers could send money home to their families. She proved that, if they were given a chance, soldiers were not the dirty, dishonest, drunken creatures they were often supposed to be, but good, clean, respectable men.

At last it was all over. The time came for Florence to return home. In England, all kinds of plans were made. The Government offered to bring her home in state in a warship. Receptions were planned at the ports where she might land. Florence would have none of it. She had done what God had called her to do, and she wanted nothing in return. She hated public affairs, where she might have to make speeches, and was determined that if anyone were to be welcomed back to England it should be the soldiers who had fought and suffered, and not herself.

*　　*　　*

One August morning in 1856, nearly two years after Florence had left England for the Crimea, the Nightingale family were sitting quietly in their Derbyshire home at Lea Hurst. They were talking of Florence, as they always seemed to be doing, wondering when she would be coming home and whether they would all be asked to go to London for her official welcome. In the distance, they had heard the sound of the train pulling into the station some distance away, and watched the smoke curl above the trees as it pulled out again. In a room at the front of the house, the housekeeper sat sewing. Now and again she looked through the open window at the park and the fields, green and gold in the summer sunshine. As she looked she saw a figure come round the bend in the drive. It was a woman.

The housekeeper put down her sewing. She was not expecting anyone to arrive, and wondered who it could be. She looked more closely as the woman drew nearer, noticing that she was dressed in black, and carried a heavy carpet-bag.

"It can't be . . ." she said to herself. Then she rushed to the door, her long skirts sweeping the carpets. She knocked sharply and burst into the room where the Nightingales were sitting. "Mrs. Nightingale, ma'am . . . Miss Parthe! It's Miss Florence! She come home all by herself on the train, and she's walking up the drive."

9

FLORENCE MEETS THE QUEEN

FLORENCE was not a sentimental person nor easily moved. She did not often get excited or lose control of herself. But even *her* hand was trembling when she came into Fanny's room one morning, not very long after she arrived back in England. She was carrying a letter. Since she received a great many letters every day, her mother did not think it could be anything special, until she looked at her face.

"Why *ever* are you looking like that, Florence?" she asked, getting up and coming towards her. "Is it . . . is it something important?"

"How do I get to Balmoral from here in Derbyshire?"

"Balmoral?" Fanny looked astonished. "I don't know. By train part way, I suppose, and then by a carriage. But why Balmoral? That is where the dear Queen is staying."

"Yes," said Florence quietly.

"Florence!" Fanny could hardly get the words out. "You are not . . . you are not going to see the Queen?"

"Yes, I am." Florence smiled rather uncertainly. "At least, this letter asks me to go to Balmoral because she wants to see me." She sat down suddenly on a straight-backed chair. "I can hardly believe it, Mother. I knew she sent messages to me through Sidney Herbert but this—well, this is quite different."

"But how wonderful!" Fanny rushed to the door, talking as she did so. "You must have lots of new clothes, of course." She opened the door and called. "Parthe! Come here, quickly. Florence is going to see the Queen!"

* * *

She was not really well, for after reaching Lea Hurst she had had to rest for some time. Her work in the Crimea had nearly killed her, and for the rest of her life she was always to be something of an invalid. The journey to Balmoral, first by train, and then by a carriage to the cottage where the Queen had arranged for her to stay, was long and tiring but, although she always took life calmly, it was exciting, too. She wondered what the Queen would look like, remembering her as she had first seen her at the London parties in the year of her wedding to Prince Albert.

Queen Victoria, when she met her, was charming. Florence would never forget driving in the carriage which the Queen had sent for her towards the lovely, fairylike castle, set amongst the Scottish hills. Nor would she forget the moment when she entered the royal presence. The Queen herself, only a year older than Florence, was sitting very upright on a sofa, while Prince Albert stood, handsome and dignified, behind her. He came towards her as she entered the door.

"My *dear* Miss Nightingale," said the Queen. "this is a moment to which I have been looking forward for a very long time." She pointed to a chair near the sofa. "Let Miss Nightingale sit *there*, Albert, where we can talk comfortably. I want to hear *all* about your work. Tell me, were the hospitals *really* dreadful when you arrived?"

In a moment or two Florence was completely at her ease. She answered question after question, and her shyness was gone before the first few minutes were over. It was clear that the Queen had followed her work very closely.

"People have admired you so *much*, Miss Nightingale. You know, everywhere there have been pictures of you."

"And even china ornaments," put in Prince Albert, "have been sold by the hundred. But I'm afraid some of them don't look in the least like you," he laughed.

"And this fund which has been raised for you," added the Queen. "All kinds of people gave money to it. I am told that every soldier in the

Army gave a day's pay towards it. What are you going to do with it?"

Not long before Florence had returned home from the Crimea, a Thanksgiving Fund had been started so that a present might be given to her when she came back. There was so much money that it was impossible to spend it on a gift for her, and she was asked to accept the money itself and to use it in any way she liked. It was one of the things that had worried her. She certainly could not use it for herself, and in any case she had plenty of money of her own. "I don't know, your Majesty," she answered. "There is a great deal of money, and I'm not sure yet what is the best way to use it."

"I am told there is over £45,000 in the Nightingale Fund," said Prince Albert. "You can't very well just give it away again, can you?"

"God will show me what to do with it when the time comes," Florence answered quietly.

*   *   *

In the days that followed, Florence saw a good deal of the Queen, for she went several times to Balmoral and, one afternoon, Queen Victoria came to the cottage in her own carriage and took her for a long walk across the moors. They talked about the Army, and Florence outlined some of the things she wanted done to make the life of the soldiers happier and easier. The Queen was always interested in what she had to say and, partly because of her interest, and because she told the Prime Minister that she expected him to listen to what Florence had to say, conditions for the British Army in every part of the world were made easier before many years had passed. When she left Balmoral to return to London she felt that she could easily give the rest of her life to helping the soldiers if God wanted her to do so. She soon found out, however, that He wanted her to do something else.

She had still kept up her friendship with "Clarkey" and the Herberts, and one day she had news for them. "I know now what God wants me to do with the Nightingale Fund," she said. "He has spoken to me again, quite clearly. Not through somebody else. I heard His voice just as I heard it when He first called me, when he sent me to Harley Street and when He told me He wanted me to go to the Crimea."

"Well?"

"I am going to use the money to train nurses for the hospitals in England."

"Well," said Sidney Herbert, "you have certainly proved to everyone that nursing can be a great profession."

"Not to *everyone*," Florence answered. "Most mothers wouldn't want their daughters to be nurses—and I don't blame them when I think what English hospitals are like. They are nearly as bad as the ones in the Crimea. The doctors don't all want well-trained nurses, either, though you might think they would." Her face took on its old determined look. "But I'm going to make everyone in England see that nursing is one of the greatest professions in the world."

*   *   *

It was not easy to find a hospital which would do as she wanted, but at last St. Thomas's Hospital, in London, agreed that when its premises were rebuilt there should be a "School for Nurses", where they could be trained according to Florence's own ideas and by her money. A lady whom she herself chose, Mrs. Wardroper, was appointed as matron, and kept the post for twenty-seven years.

Florence had been right, as she usually was. There was a great deal of opposition to her idea of training nurses instead of merely taking any woman who was willing to help for a miserable wage and knew nothing at all about the causes or treatment of disease. By this time, however, Florence was used to fighting for her own way, though she usually persuaded people to accept what she thought right rather than argued about it. Her nurses, in the first year, were very few, but they were the best that could be chosen out of all who applied for admission to the School. They were young, instead of middle-aged, hard-working instead of careless, and in their neat brown uniforms, with white caps and aprons, they looked charming and efficient. It was expected that they would train for a year, and then be sent to other hospitals where they would begin to teach others by their example and their work what good nursing was really like.

"It won't work," said most people. "They'll be running off to get married as soon as they've finished their training." That, at least, did not happen. Mrs. Wardroper kept too sharp an eye on them, and Florence expected a confidential report on each one every month.

"These girls will be giving *us* orders before long, instead of the other way round," grumbled some of the old doctors. "They walk round as if they owned the hospital. The only things a nurse needs to know is how to put on a poultice—and they can soon learn *that*! Training for nursing, indeed!"

By the end of the first year, the doctors were changing their minds, and after two or three years "Nightingale nurses" were in demand all over the country. There were not enough to send to all the places which asked for them. Florence had to keep an eye on their work from a distance by this time, for she was never really well, and often spent weeks in bed. She never lost touch with them, however, and expected them to write to her and let her know what they were doing. At the same time, she was busy advising the War Office about clothing for soldiers going to India and the East, stables for the horses belonging to the cavalry regiment, medical supplies for hospitals and a hundred different things. The American Government sent to her for advice about their own problems in the Army. All kinds of people in England who were anxious to improve the conditions of the hospitals and work-houses kept her answering letters or suggesting improvements. She wrote a book on "home nursing" for housewives. When Henri Dunant, the founder of the Red Cross, came to London to speak about his great work in founding that wonderful society he began by saying: "It is to an English woman that all the honour is due . . . what inspired me was the work of Miss Florence Nightingale in the Crimea. . ."

If Florence was well-known in England by the end of the Crimean War, she had become, twenty years later, one of the most famous women in the world.

10

THE NIGHTINGALE LEGEND

OUT of the doors of the old St. Thomas's Hospital the nurses came streaming into the streets of London. The roads were gay with flags and bunting. Everywhere there were crowds of people, dressed in their best clothes. Some had been waiting for hours, and a few had been in their places all night long. They were there to greet old Queen Victoria, who had reigned for fifty years. This was her Jubilee year, 1887, and she was to ride through the streets of London in her coach. She very seldom appeared now in public, and the "Nightingale nurses" were coming to join the throngs which would cheer her as she rode slowly along.

*   *   *

Florence Nightingale, too, was an old lady, almost as old as the Queen. She, too, seldom left her home, though she went now and again to see her friends. To the nurses of the Jubilee year she was almost a legend already. In her home, with its light paint, its uncurtained windows looking out on to the green lawns, its masses of flowers in vases and pots, she ruled her servants and her friends quietly and kindly. Her old fighting spirit had given way to a gentler mood. She had grown stouter, and her hair was white. Her work, however, still went on. Whenever a nurse left the Training School, Florence expected to see her and talk to her. When her nurses were ill she sent them away to the country or the sea to get better. When they went to take up a new post they found flowers in their rooms to greet them, sent by Florence, the "Lady in Chief". There was a great deal she wanted still to do, though she wondered if she would have the time to get it all done. Sometimes she wondered, too, about the money it would need.

Important visitors to England went to see her, and she had special receptions for royalty now and again, but most of all she loved to see little children, and her old friends.

"You've done so much," they said to her.

"Yes," she answered. "I think I have. There are sixteen hospitals now where the matrons are old Nightingale nurses."

"And you've sent parties of your nurses, to help in training others, all over the world."

The old lady nodded. "Yes," she said quietly, "all over the world. To Australia, and Canada, the United States, India, Ceylon, Germany. I can

hardly count up the countries they've gone to."
She stroked the cat gently which was curled up on
her lap. "But there's something else I want to do.
I want to start a scheme for training nurses to look
after old people and poor people in their own
homes."

"But there are the hospitals for them to go to.
No one need be afraid of going to them now—
they're so different from what they used to be."

"That's true. But not everyone can go to hospital when they're sick. There wouldn't be enough
room. And not everyone is ill enough to go. No,
no. They need nurses to look after them at home—
when their babies are born, for instance. *District*
nurses. But I don't know whether there will be
enough money to do what I want."

The answer to her newest dream came quickly
and surprisingly. All over the Empire people sent
money as a Thanksgiving present to the Queen,
for her to use in any way she liked. A message
came to Florence one day which made her hand
shake. She remembered how it had shaken once
before when she had had a letter asking her to go
to Balmoral to meet the Queen. Now there was
another message from the Queen. This time it did
not ask her to meet her—they both felt too old
for that. The letter told Florence that the Queen
had decided to give the money which had come
into her Jubilee Fund to start a home to train the

"District Nurses" which Florence had been so eager to start. It was a wonderful moment. It meant the beginning of something new for Florence to think about and plan. The "Jubilee Institute for Nurses" was the result.

Florence thanked God for the way He had used her gifts. She did not often talk about God, for she never found that easy. Her faith was a very personal matter, but those who knew her best knew how deeply she loved God. She had never taken a decision without praying about it. She had never fought her battles alone, but always in His strength. If, at the end of her life, she knew that she had achieved more than she had ever dreamed possible, she knew too that it was because God had called her and she had been ready to answer His call, wherever it led. The work would go on when she was gone.

*　　*　　*

Down the steps of the new St. Thomas's Hospital, overlooking the Thames, the nurses still stream into the streets of London. Inside the hospital is the "Crimea carriage" which Florence used in her last months as she toured round the battlefields. In the hospital, too, is a sash, embroidered with the word *Scutari*. The wards are quiet now and the operating theatres—so different from the screens and tables in the Barrack Hospital at Scutari—are busy. Nursing has become a great and honourable profession. Out of the hospital doors come the nurses, in their caps and neat uniforms, with their red cloaks flying behind them in the breeze, the latest recruits to the great army which the "Lady in Chief" once led. Florence herself died in 1910, but the work she began will go on as long as there are men, women and children in any part of the world who are in need.